ou

HEY!
SOMEONE'S
WATCHING US!

GUYS, COME HERE.
LOOK AT THIS.

THERE ARE
PEOPLE HERE . . .
AND THEY'VE OPENED
OUR BOOK!
3

Hi THERE.
WHO ARE YOU?
WHAT DO YOU WANT

YOU'RE VERY SWEET.
WOW!

SO, WHAT NOW?
I THINK THEY WOULD LIKE A STORY.

WHAT?
HOW ARE WE SUPPOSED
TO DO THAT?
COULD YOU
MAYBE
COME BACK
LATER?
ER, YES, THAT
WOULD BE GREAT.
WE'RE NOT QUITE
READY YET, YOU SEE.

WE COULD TRY
ADDING A BIT OF
BACKGROUND COLOR.

OOH, GOOD IDEA. THAT WOULD MAKE
EVERYTHING MUCH PRETTIER.
AND NEATER.

MAYBE THEY'D LIKE
A LANDSCAPE?
I'LL GO
FIND ONE!
YEAH,
IT'S REALLY
MESSY HERE.

WELL?

Is THAT
BETTER?
How is iT?

HMMM, WE'RE
BORING YOU,
AREN'T WE?
SORRY!

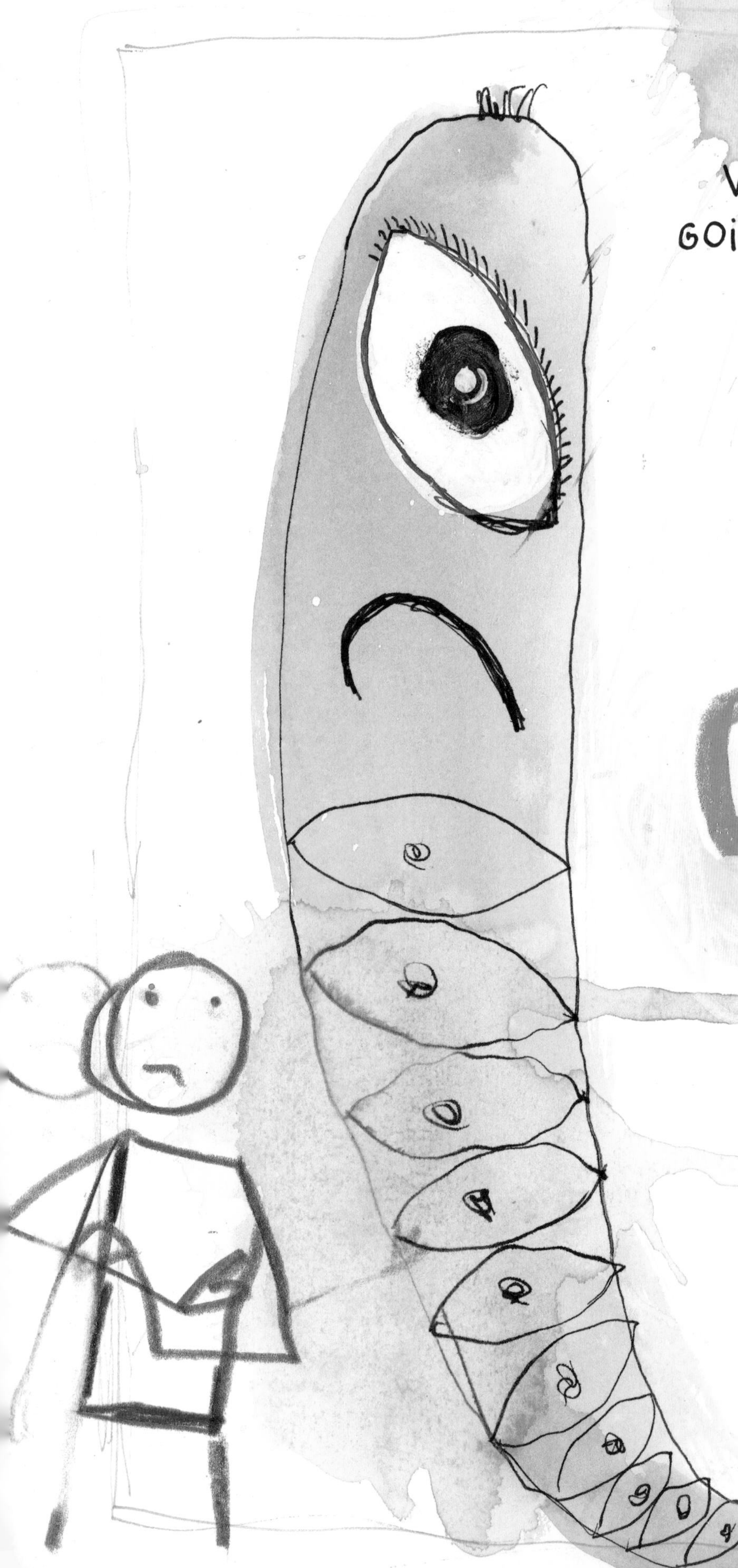

WHAT ARE WE
GOING TO DO NOW?

WELL . . .
SOMETIMES IN STORIES,
THERE'S A BAD GUY.

HEY, YOU, BAD GUY! COME HERE!
YES— GOOD iDEA!

BO

O!

NOW WHAT?

CAN'T YOU SEE
THERE ARE PEOPLE HERE?
YOU'RE SUPPOSED TO SCARE THEM!

OOH, YES, HELLO THERE!
AREN'T YOU SWEET?

I COULD JUST EAT YOU UP!

DO YOU
HAVE AN IDEA
FOR A STORY
OR NOT?
IF NOT, THE VERY SWEET
PEOPLE WILL LEAVE.
BECAUSE THE THING
IS, WE'RE STILL NOT
READY FOR THEM.
YOU CAN SAY
THAT AGAIN.

A STORY? I DON'T KNOW ANYTHING ABOUT STORIES. BUT I DO KNOW IT ISN'T EASY TO MAKE ONE. YOU'RE GOING TO NEED SOMEONE ELSE . . . AN AUTHOR!

REALLY?
WHAT DOES AN AUTHOR DO?

AND WHERE
CAN WE FIND ONE?

OH, DEAR,
SOME STORY THIS IS
TURNING OUT TO BE.

HEY!
YOU'RE RIGHT!
WAIT!
WE KNOW AN AUTHOR!

HEY, AUTHOR !!!!!

YOU'LL SEE.
THIS AUTHOR IS
MUCH BETTER AT
MAKING UP STORIES
THAN WE ARE.

YEAH, HE'S NOT BAD.
WE JUST HAVEN'T SEEN HIM
IN A LONG TIME!

HEY, AUTHOR!
EVERY

BODY'S HERE!

AUTHO

R!!!
HERVÉ
TULLET*

OH, HELLO!
HERVÉ
TULLET*

UH-
OH!
HE DOESN'-
LOOK TOO
HAPPY.

UM, HOW DID
YOU GET IN HERE?

SORRY, BUT YOU CAN'T STAY HERE. I'M NOT READY. THIS BOOK ISN'T FINISHED YET!

But they **WANT** a story!

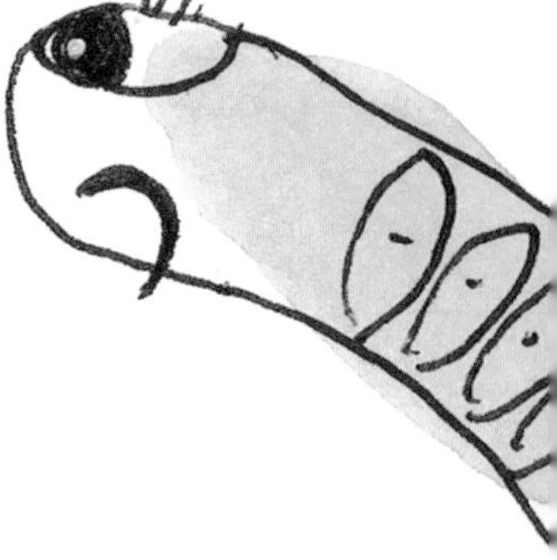

You could at least **TRY**!

They've come so far!

They're really nice, too. . . .

And they did actually CHOOSE our book!

FINE, FINE.
JUST ONE STORY. ONE TEENY, TINY STORY . . .
AND THEN YOU GUYS HAVE TO GET OUT OF HERE, OK?

YIPPEE!
A STORY!
AT LAST!
HOORAY!

ALL RIGHT, THEN.

Once upon a time,
on a beautiful sunny day, our heroes were walking peacefully along a road, when, all of a sudden . . .

a monster attacked them!

But the beautiful, kind fairy, who knew a magic spell
and had a magic wand, said, "Beat it, bad guy!"

And the evil monster ~~left~~ ~~took off~~ disappeared!

WHOO-HOO! IT WORKED!

WILL THAT DO?

AT LEAST
WE LOOK GOOD
IN THE PICTURES.

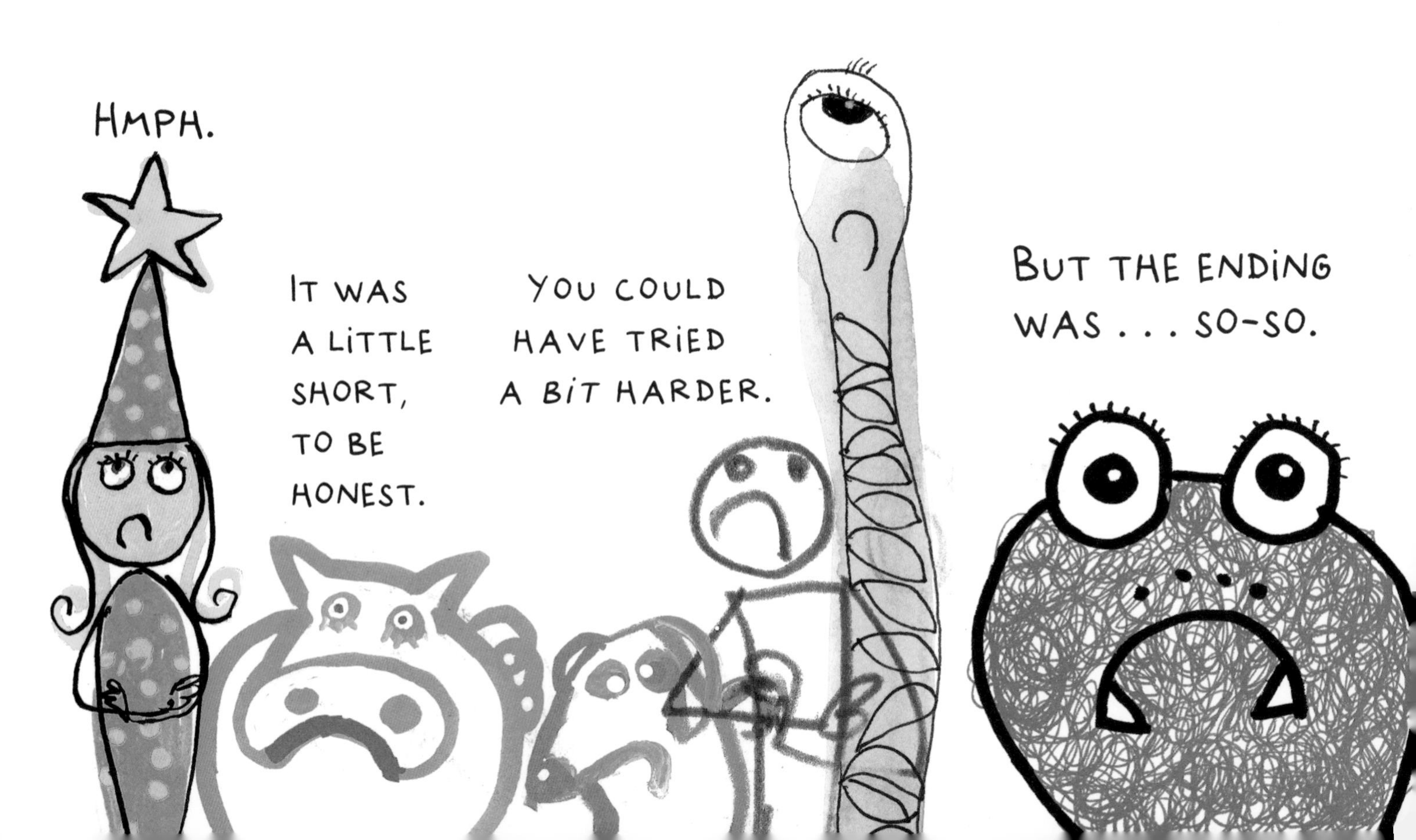

HMPH.
IT WAS A LITTLE SHORT, TO BE HONEST.
YOU COULD HAVE TRIED A BIT HARDER.
BUT THE ENDING WAS . . . SO-SO.

IT WAS SO-SO?

LOOK, IF YOU'RE NOT HAPPY, YOU CAN GO AND LOOK FOR A STORY SOMEWHERE ELSE.

THERE ARE LOTS OF OTHER BOOKS, YOU KNOW!

AND BEFORE YOU LEAVE, COULD YOU DO ME A LITTLE FAVOR, DEAR READER?

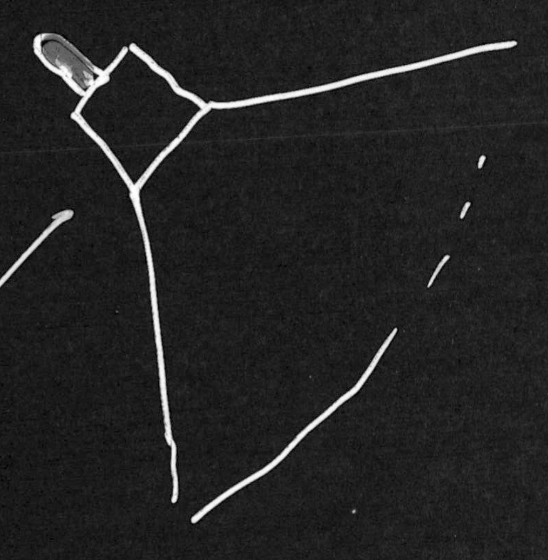

THANK YOU!

AND IF YOU SEE ANY OTHER READERS, PLEASE TELL THEM NOT TO CHOOSE THIS BOOK!

NOT YET, ANYWAY. AT LEAST NOT UNTIL WE HAVE A TITLE.

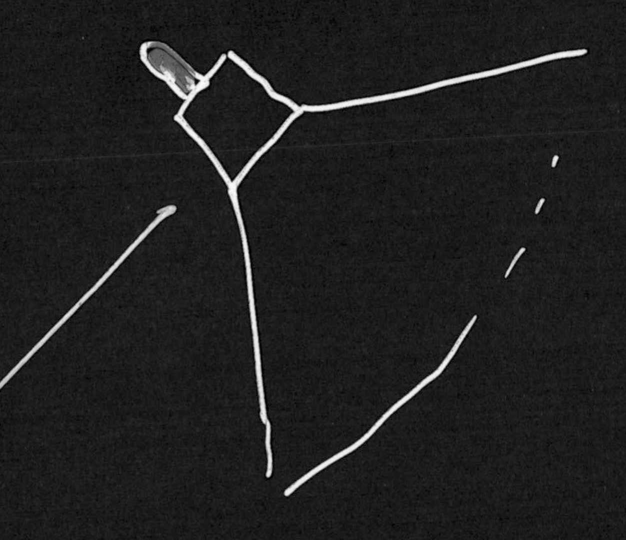

HEY, READERS,
CAN YOU PLEASE
TURN THE LIGHT
BACK ON?

I'LL DO IT —
GIVE ME A SEC.

WELL, THE AUTHOR
DIDN'T SEEM
TOO HAPPY.

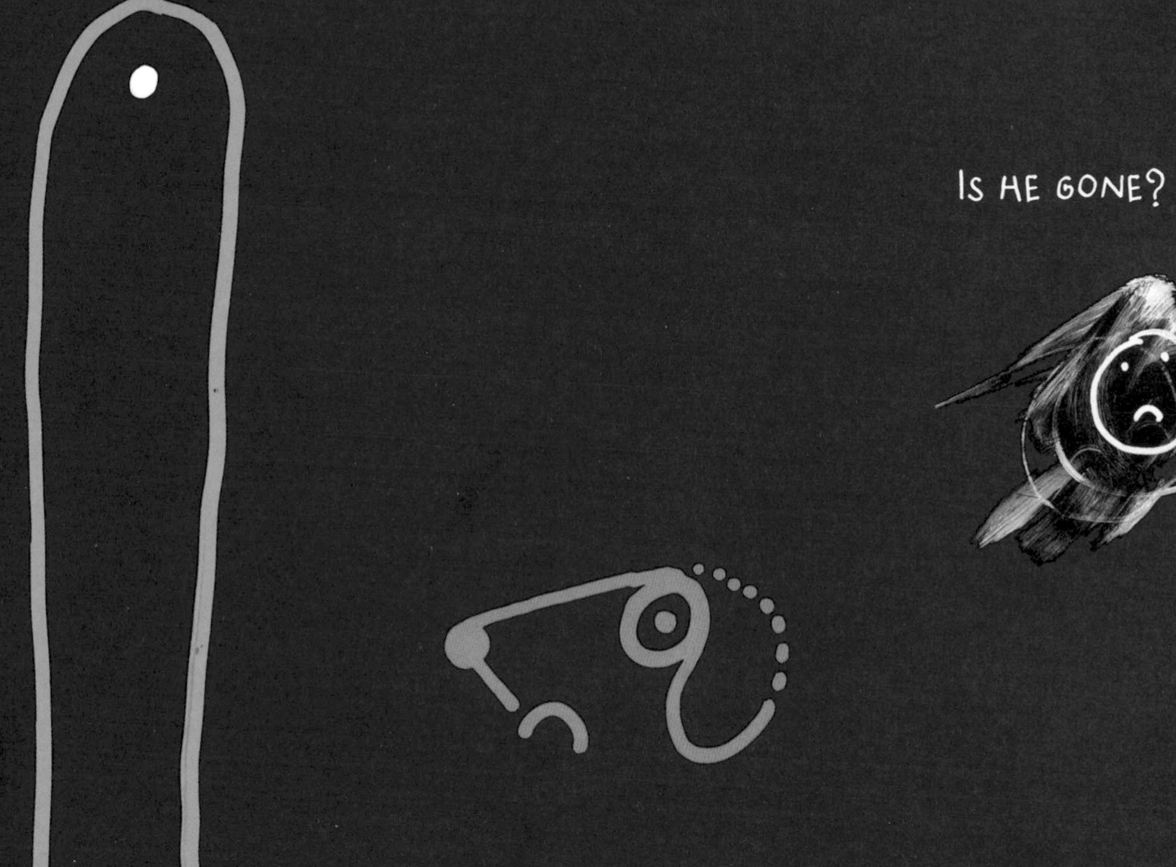

IS HE GONE?

THANKS.
PHEW.

YEAH, IT WAS PRETTY COOL WHAT HE DID.

WE SHOULDN'T BE TOO HARD ON THE AUTHOR. WE DID CATCH HIM OFF GUARD.

BUT WHAT ARE WE GOING TO DO NOW?

WELL, THERE ARE ONLY A FEW PAGES LEFT. SO . . .

HOW ABOUT
GOOD-BYE THEN?
YES,
GOOD-BYE!

THANKS
FOR COMING.

SEE YOU!

HMMM . . .

WANNA PLAY?
34

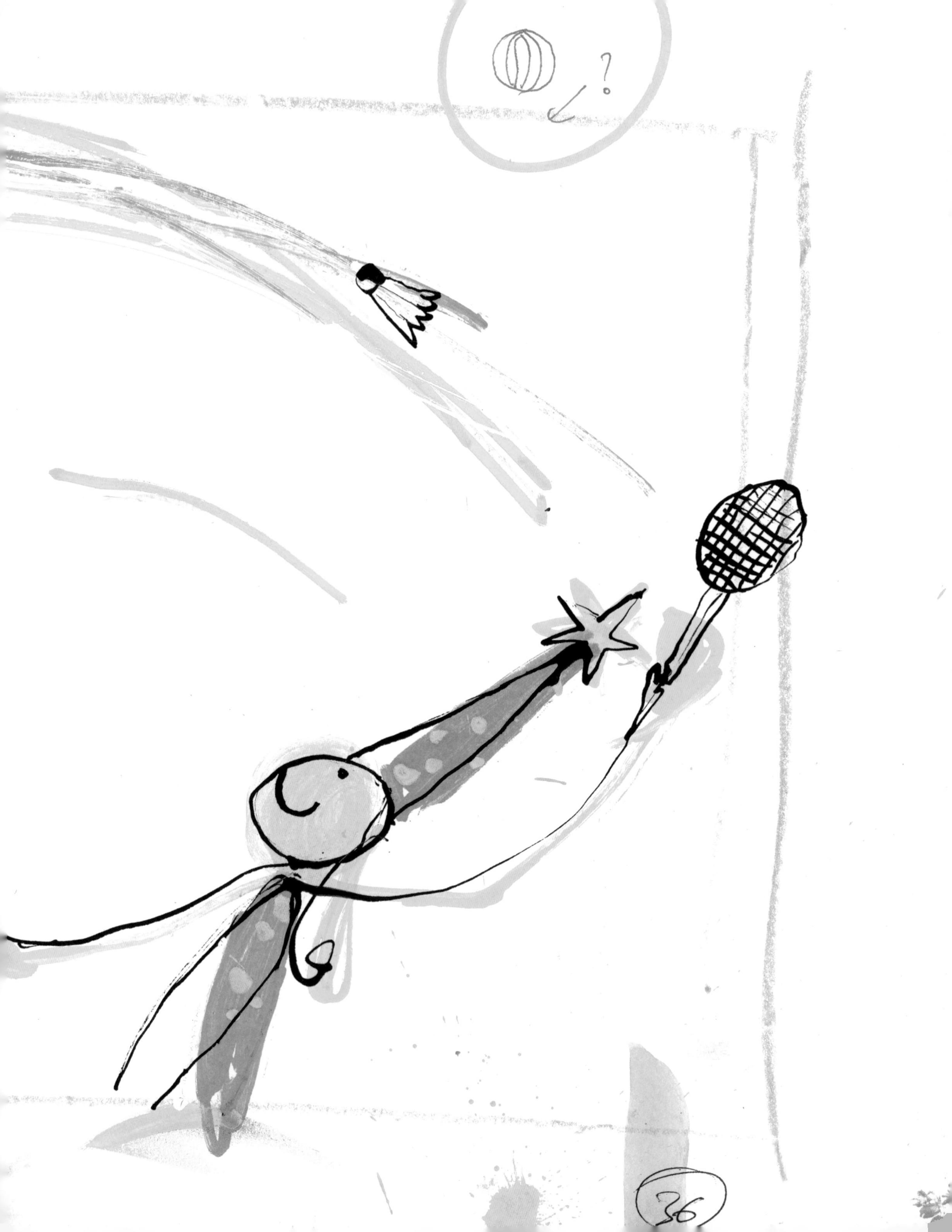

THE END

Originally published in France
by Bayard Éditions S.A. under the title *Sans Titre*

First U.S. edition 2014

Library of Congress Catalog Card Number 2013944015
ISBN 978-0-7636-7021-4

14 15 16 17 18 19 TLF
1 2 3 4 5 6 7 8 9 10

Printed in Dongguan, Guangdong, China

This book was typeset in Hervé Tullet Whimsy.
The illustrations were done in mixed media.

Candlewick Press
99 Dover Street
Somerville, Massachusetts 02144

visit us at www.candlewick.com

HERVÉ TULLET
MAY NOT HAVE FINISHED THIS BOOK,
BUT HE HAS FINISHED MANY OTHERS, INCLUDING

PRESS HERE,

WHICH HAS BEEN TRANSLATED INTO
THIRTY THREE LANGUAGES
AND MADE INTO AN APP.

HERVÉ TULLET LIVES IN PARIS AND IS
CELEBRATED THE WORLD OVER
FOR HIS PLAYFUL, INVENTIVE,
AND INTERACTIVE STORYTELLING.